FERGUS in the PARK

Dedicated to
Cannon Hill Park, Birmingham,
where as a child I enjoyed
many happy family outings.

MYRIAD BOOKS LIMITED
35 Bishopsthorpe Road, London SE26 4PA

First published in 2006 by
PICCADILLY PRESS LIMITED
5 Castle Road, London NW1 8PR
www.piccadillypress.co.uk

ISBN 1 84746 119 0
EAN 9 781847 461193

Designed by Tony Maddox and Simon Davis

Printed in China

FERGUS in the PARK

Tony Maddox

MYRIAD BOOKS LIMITED

Fergus was waiting in
the truck for Farmer Bob.
It was a warm, sunny day.

He could see the park across the street.
It looked cool and inviting.

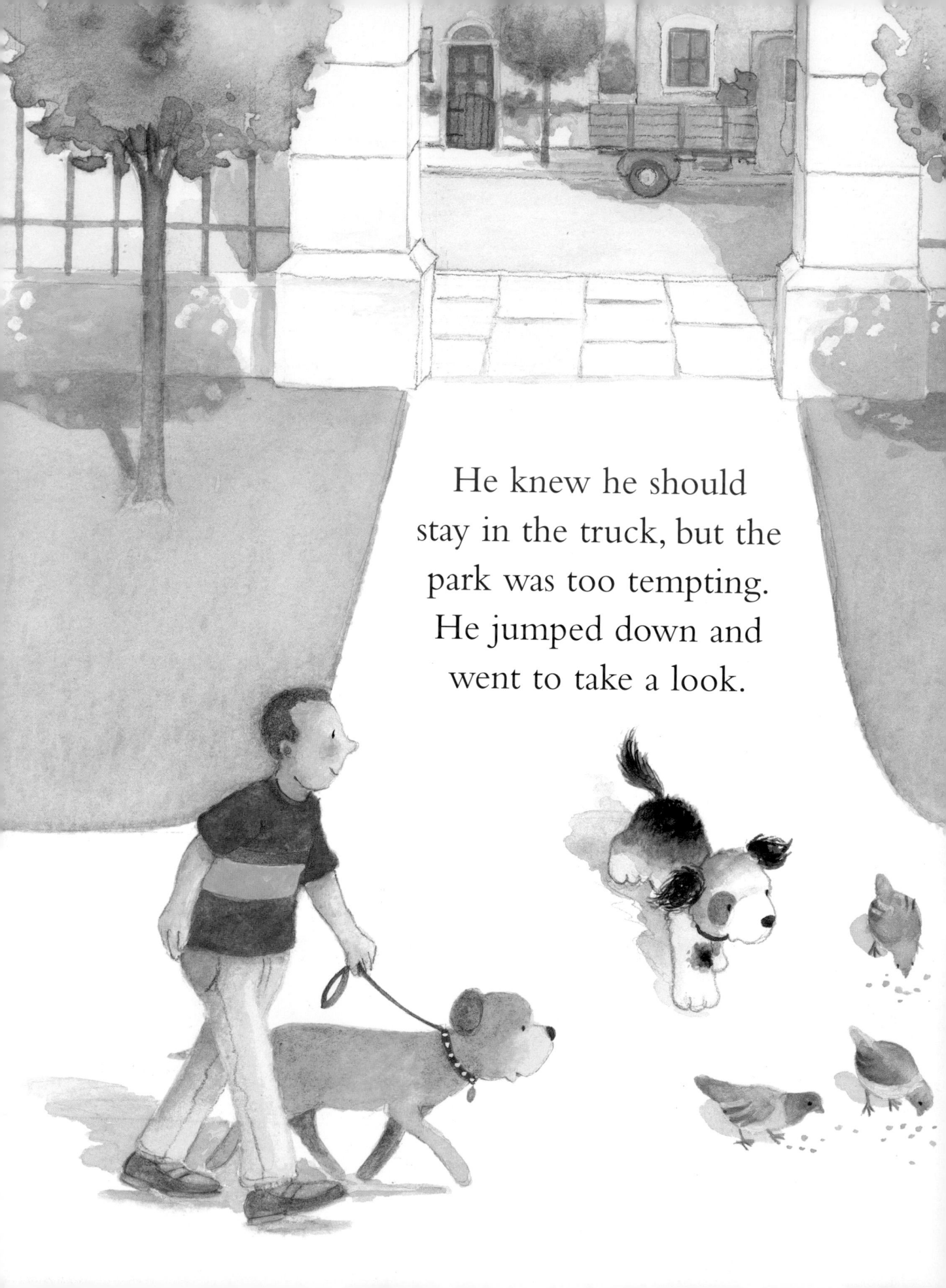

He knew he should
stay in the truck, but the
park was too tempting.
He jumped down and
went to take a look.

"This is better than sitting in the back of Farmer Bob's old truck," he thought, as he strolled through the trees.

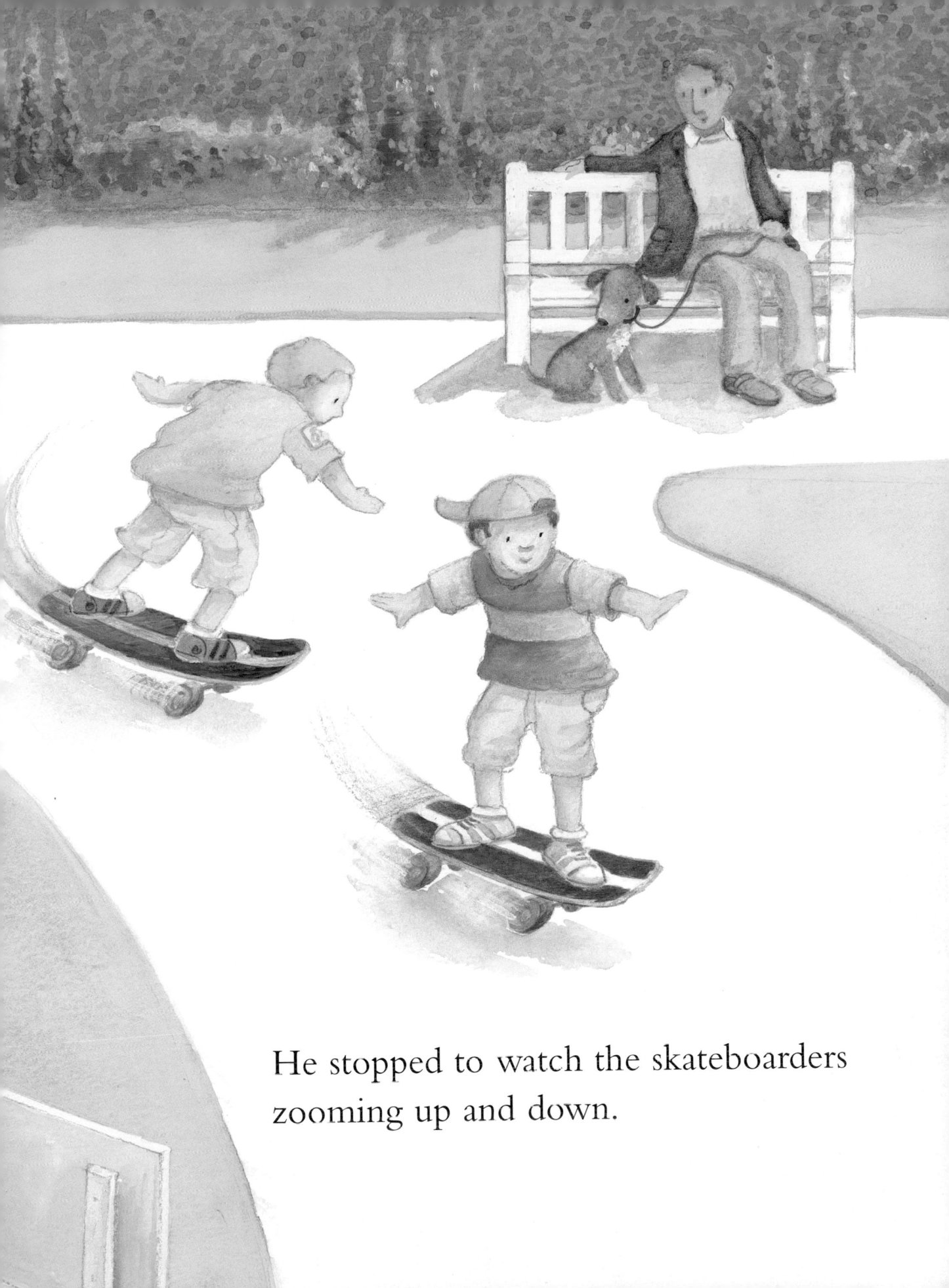

He stopped to watch the skateboarders
zooming up and down.

He began to imagine that he
was a champion skateboarder,
performing all sorts of tricks.
Wouldn't that be fun?

His daydreams were broken by
an angry shout behind him.

He turned to see the park keeper
hurrying towards him.

DOGS MUST BE ON LEADS

"Can't you read?" he demanded,
pointing to a large sign.
Fergus was puzzled.
"What a silly question," he thought.
"Of course I can't read. I'm a dog!"

In this situation, the best thing to do was ...

RUN!

Through the park he raced, with the park
keeper close behind. Other dogs, excited by
all the commotion, broke loose from their
owners and joined in the chase.

The park keeper was getting closer and closer.
"He's going to catch me!" groaned Fergus.

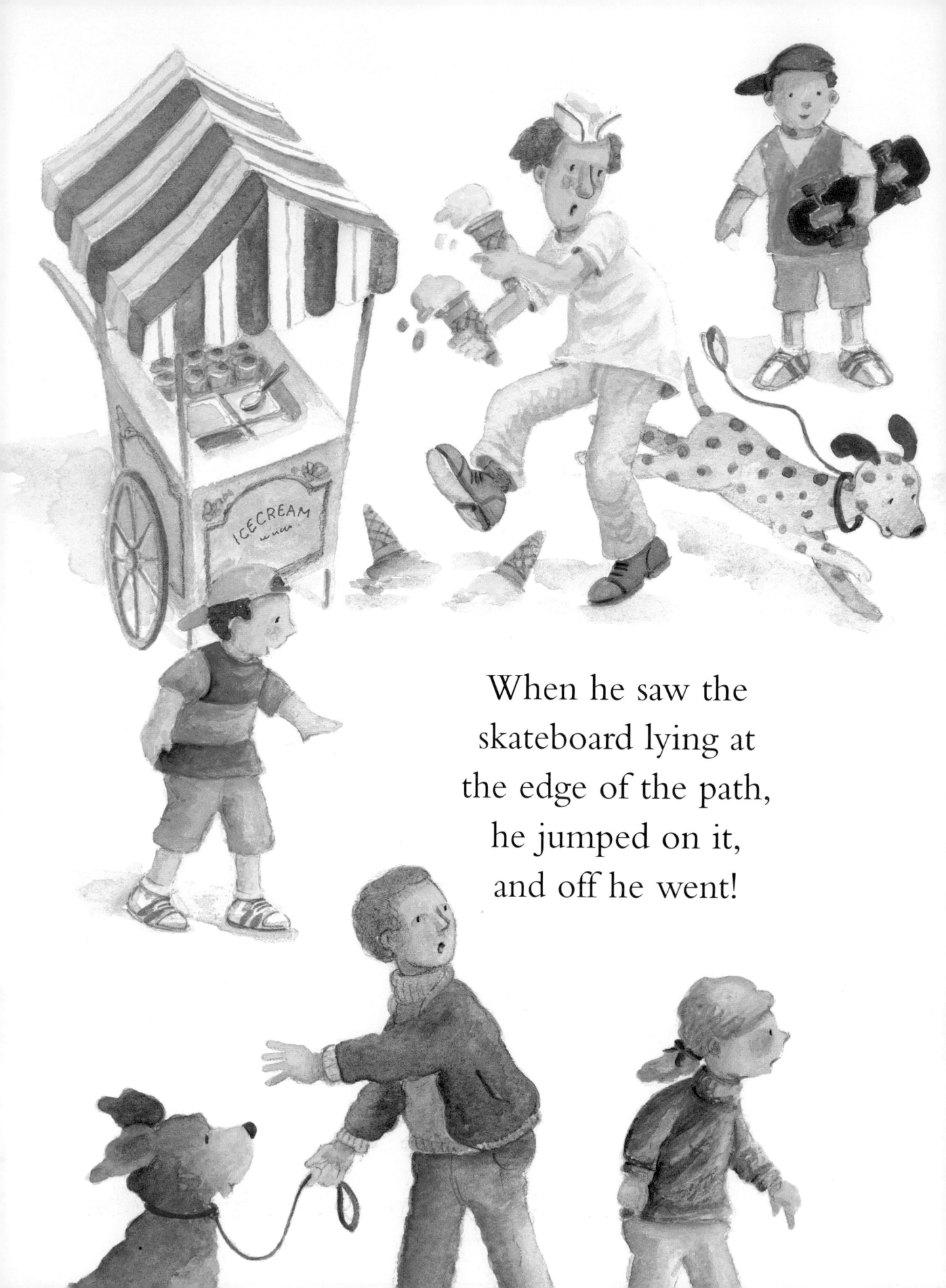

When he saw the
skateboard lying at
the edge of the path,
he jumped on it,
and off he went!

People scattered as he whizzed along.

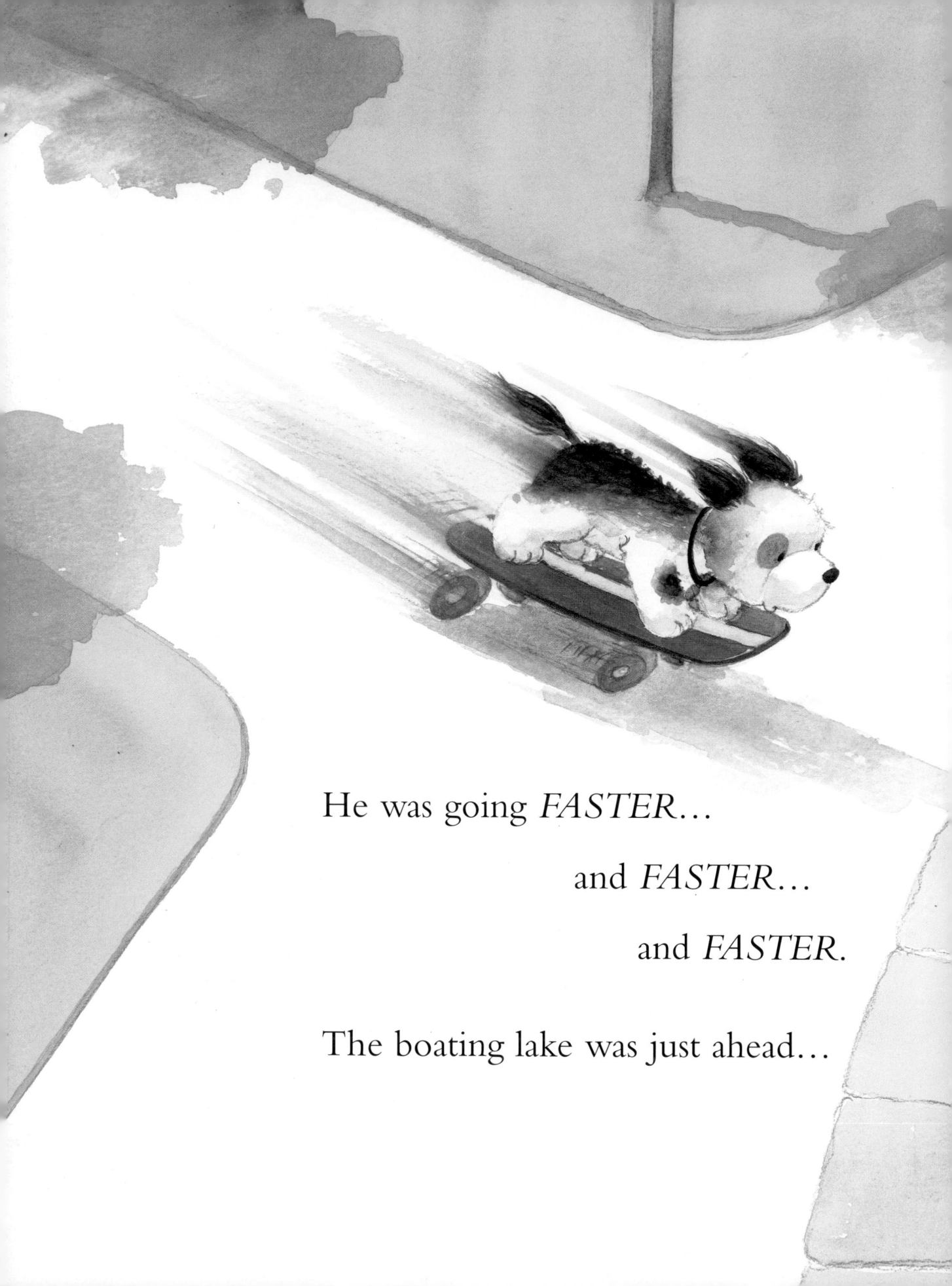

He was going *FASTER*…

and *FASTER*…

and *FASTER*.

The boating lake was just ahead…

Boats
for
HIRE

HOW WAS HE GOING TO STOP?

Too late! There he was…
flying UP…UP…UP into the air…
and then *down…down …down*

into the lake with a great *BIG SPLASH!*

He began to swim towards the
island in the middle of the lake.
"I'll be safe there," he gasped.

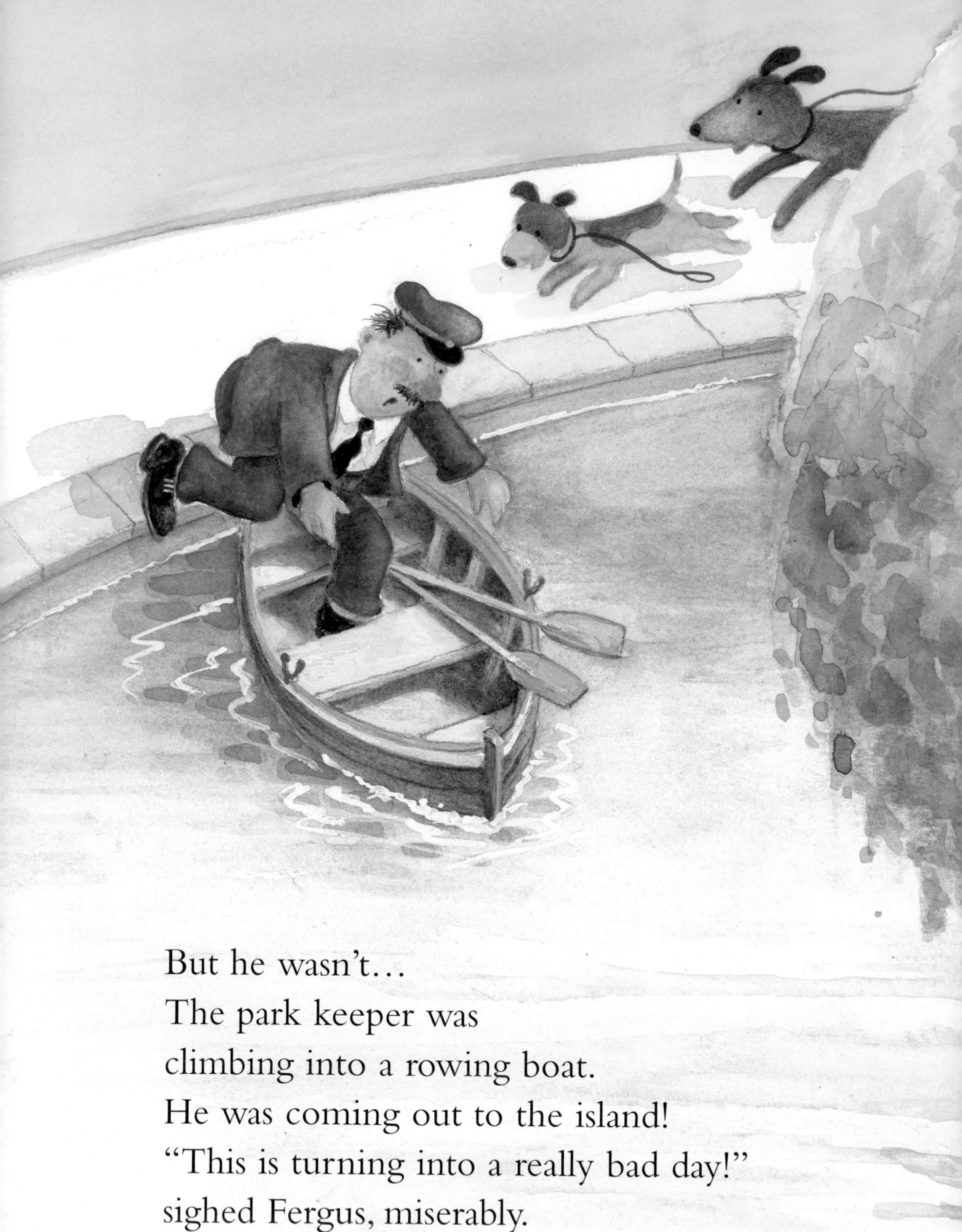

But he wasn't...
The park keeper was
climbing into a rowing boat.
He was coming out to the island!
"This is turning into a really bad day!"
sighed Fergus, miserably.

But help was at hand.
The ducks who lived on the island
thought of a way Fergus could escape
without the park keeper knowing.

Together, with Fergus hidden in the middle,
they paddled slowly past the park keeper
and back to the park.

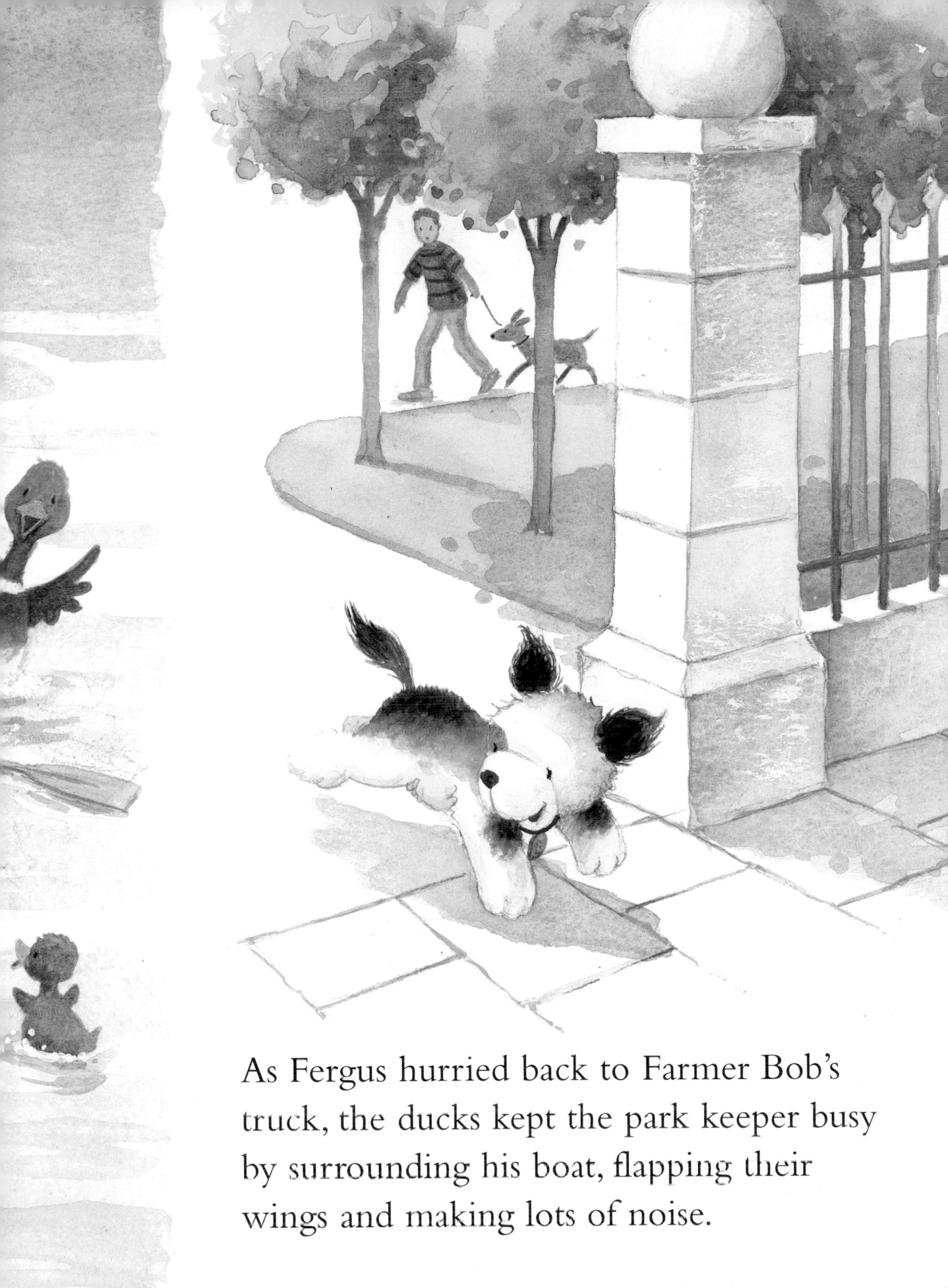

As Fergus hurried back to Farmer Bob's truck, the ducks kept the park keeper busy by surrounding his boat, flapping their wings and making lots of noise.

"Sorry I've taken so long, Fergus,"
said Farmer Bob when he returned.

"I know! As you've been so good,
we'll go for a walk in the park!"